Hats, Hats, Hats
Sombreros, sombreros, sombreros

by Deborah Schecter

ISBN: 978-1-338-70287-3
Illustrated by Anne Kennedy
Copyright © 2020 by Deborah Schecter. All rights reserved.
Published by Scholastic Inc., 557 Broadway, New York, NY 10012

10 9 8 7 6   68   23 24 25 26/0

Printed in Jiaxing, China. First printing, June 2020.

I have a hat that is tall.

Tengo un sombrero alto.

I have a hat that is small.

Tengo un sombrero pequeño.

I have a hat that has holes.

Tengo un sombrero con agujeros.

I have a hat that rolls.

Tengo un sombrero que rueda.

I have a hat that flops.

Tengo un sombrero que cae.

I have a hat that is a mop.

Tengo un sombrero que es
un trapeador.

Hats, hats, hats.
I like hats a lot!

Sombreros, sombreros, sombreros.
¡Me encantan los sombreros!